Ajo 'pi sann avyayatma bhutanam isvaro 'pi san
Prakritim svam adhishthaya sambhavamy atma-mayaya

My true being is unborn and changeless. I am the Lord who
dwells in every creature. Through the power of my own maya,
I manifest myself in a finite form.

Sri Krishna to Arjuna, Bhagvad Gita, Chapter 4, Verse 6

To my friend Hari

For making this Series possible!

anjana
publishing

Second Edition, June 2015

House L, Orient Crest, 76 Peak Road, The Peak, Hong Kong

ISBN: 978-988-12394-5-7

Designed by Jump Web Services Ltd.
Production by Macmillan Production (Asia) Ltd.
Tracking Code CP-06/15
Printed in Guangdong Province China
This book is printed on paper made from well-managed sustainable forest sources.

Amma, Tell Me

How Krishna Defeated Kansa!

Part 3 in the Krishna Trilogy

Written by
Bhakti Mathur

Illustrated by
Maulshree Somani

They settled down on the swing,

A few early stars lit the evening sky.

Klaka and Kiki's eyes were on Amma.

"Ready, boys?" she asked, putting down her 'chai'.

She smiled and said, "Since you both

Are always ready for a new story,

Let me tell you some more tales

About young Krishna's rise to glory.

Krishna was now a handsome young lad
With curly hair and a mischievous smile.
His eyes were as beautiful as lotus petals,
He wore a peacock feather in his hair for style.

He loved singing and dancing with his friends,
But playing his flute is what he liked doing best -
Mesmerizing the 'gopis' with enchanting tunes,
They would dance with joy for hours without rest.

All of Vrindavan loved him dearly
For he was their saviour - brave and strong.
Ready to take on ferocious demons,
And anyone who was evil and did wrong.

And so it was, that one day when Krishna
Was playing with his friends by a lake,
Their ball fell in the water and when Krishna jumped in,
He found himself facing a ferocious, hissing snake.

This was none other than the infamous 'Kaliya':
The many headed snake, as evil as can be!

Killing those around him with his powerful venom,
Spreading havoc and making everyone flee.

Seeing Krishna he said, "This young lad
Will be a delicious meal for me.
I'm glad you fell in the lake, my boy!
Believe me, I'm terribly hungry."

Immediately Kaliya hypnotized him
With a wicked and piercing gaze.
It put Krishna under a powerful spell,
Leaving the boy in a bit of a daze.

Then Kaliya made his next move,
Twisting around Krishna inch by inch,
Trying to squeeze the life out of him,
While Krishna, so calm, did not even flinch.

The waters of the lake were so still
That Krishna's friends thought him dead.
They cried in desperation,
As they feared what lay ahead.

But under the calm waters of the lake,
Things were not as serene as they seemed,
For Krishna had escaped from Kaliya's clutches -
And suddenly someone screamed!

There was a loud splash,
And his friends turned to see
A sight that left them spellbound,
In a kind of reverie...

Kaliya and Krishna had both emerged
And Kaliya looked subdued,
For dancing merrily on his heads
Was Krishna, playing the flute!

The ferocious Kaliya had been tamed!
To the ocean Krishna banished the snake.
It was safe again for all of God's creatures
To drink water and graze by the lake.

There were other tales of bravery

That made Vrindavan love little Krishna,

And the most famous one of all was

How he fought the mighty God Indra...

Every year, the people of Vrindavan
Worshipped Indra, Lord of the Clouds.
They hoped he would send them rain,
So in front of him they bowed.

One year Krishna said, "Why pray to Indra?
Dosen't Govardhan Hill deserve our prayers instead?
For it feeds our cows with its fresh grass
And gives us meadows, trees and flowerbeds."

So Krishna led all the villagers
To the foot of Govardhan Hill,
Where they prayed and offered flowers and fruits,
Much to the Mountain's thrill.

Now Indra was arrogant and wanted
Everyone to keep worshipping him.
On seeing Vrindavan praying to Govardhan
He lost his temper and became very grim.

He decided to punish the villagers
And sent rain and thunder their way.
Vrindavan was struck with a raging storm
The villagers panicked, filled with dismay.

The village was totally flooded,
And nobody knew what to do.
Their homes and cattle were drowning;
How would they see the storm through?

Desperate, they ran to Krishna for help.
He said, "Don't worry, just follow me.
Govardhan Hill will give us shelter.
Trust, have faith, and you will see."

Trudging, they reached Govardhan Hill,
And a magical sight did unfold:
Krishna picked up the hill on his little finger;
It was such a miracle to behold!

For seven days and seven nights
On Krishna's finger stood Govardhan.
Just like a giant umbrella it shaded
The villagers and animals of Vrindavan.

Indra's plans had not worked;
The villagers were safe and shielded.
"How is it that my storm failed," he thought
"Why haven't the people of Vrindavan yielded?"

Indra arrived on his elephant,
And was shocked to see a little boy
Holding Govardhan on his fingertip,
As though he were lifting a toy.

Realising Krishna was no ordinary lad,
Indra said, "So foolish were my decrees!
In my arrogance I made a big mistake.
O Krishna, do forgive me, please."

Meanwhile in Mathura, Kansa grew more afraid
As he came to hear of Krishna's heroic tales.
He hatched another plan to kill him,
Hoping that this time he would not fail.

His messenger arrived in Vrindavan,
A royal invitation for Krishna in hand.
"His highness invites Krishna to Mathura
To honour the bravest boy in his land."

Yashoda was suspicious of Kansa's intent
She was afraid he meant Krishna harm.
She insisted that he go to Mathura
Accompanied by his foster brother, Balaram.

Her fears were right, for at the city gates,
A huge elephant blocked the brothers' path.
He was Kulavapidiya, Kansa's pet elephant,
Sent by Kansa to slay Krishna in a bloodbath.

Krishna was not afraid and caught
The elephant's tusks with all his might.
They both remained locked together
In a long and fearsome fight.

Finally the elephant grew tired;
He was beat and out of breath.
He buckled and fell with a thud
To the ground, meeting his death.

When Kansa heard the news
That his dear elephant was dead,
He called his wrestlers - Canura and Mustika
And said, "Go bring me Krishna's head."

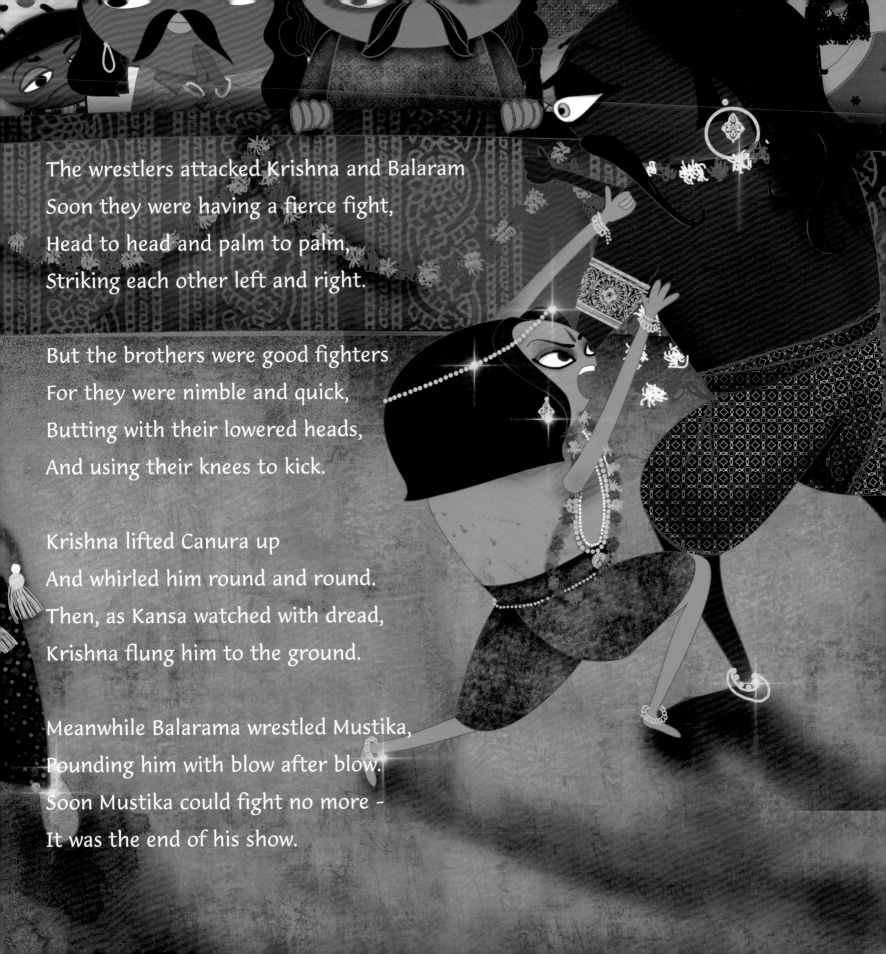

The wrestlers attacked Krishna and Balaram
Soon they were having a fierce fight,
Head to head and palm to palm,
Striking each other left and right.

But the brothers were good fighters
For they were nimble and quick,
Butting with their lowered heads,
And using their knees to kick.

Krishna lifted Canura up
And whirled him round and round.
Then, as Kansa watched with dread,
Krishna flung him to the ground.

Meanwhile Balarama wrestled Mustika,
Pounding him with blow after blow.
Soon Mustika could fight no more –
It was the end of his show.

Krishna looked to Kansa and said,
"Is this how you treat your guest?
Enough harm you have caused this land
It is time to put your evil to rest."

Krishna ran up to the throne
And pulled Kansa by his hair.
He dragged him into the arena,
Causing Kansa to gasp for air.

Krishna straddled Kansa's back
And hit him again and again,
Until Kansa, bloodied and bruised,
Took his last breath and was finally slain.

All of Mathura erupted with joy,
For they had endured years of pain.
They were now free of the tyrant,
The curtain had come down on Kansa's reign!

Krishna freed his parents Vasudev and Devaki,
And his grandfather, old Urgasena, too
After years of hardship suffered in prison,
They rejoiced to see Krishna come to their rescue.

They showered their blessings on Krishna,
Even as they shed many tears of joy.
Ugrasena then said to his grandson,
"You must now lead Mathura, my boy."

Krishna said, "I am too young
And must learn to run a kingdom.
My time will come later, grandfather.
Now this is your moment of freedom."

So Krishna crowned Ugrasena
As the true and rightful king.
And after years of sorrow,
Had all of Mathura celebrating!

So that, my dear Klaka and Kiki,
Is how Kansa's end came to be.
Krishna finally prevailed over him
And fulfilled the divine prophecy!"